# Magic
# in the
# Park

by Ruth Chew
Illustrated by the author

**SCHOLASTIC INC.**
NEW YORK   TORONTO   LONDON   AUCKLAND   SYDNEY

Reading level is determined
by the Spache Readability Formula.
2.0 signifies low second grade level.

ISBN 0-590-40119-X

12 11 10 9 8 7 6 5 4 3 2 1    8    6 7 8 9/8 0 1/9
Printed in the U.S.A.                          11

..................

*To Eve*
*who is afraid*
*of the park*

# 1

"I HATE Brooklyn! Why did we have to move here?" Jennifer threw her school books onto the kitchen table.

Her mother picked up the books and put them in a neat pile. "Daddy has a job here, Jenny," she said. "We have to live where Daddy can work."

Jennifer thought about the woods and fields near Carbondale and about the school where everybody knew everybody else. "Mother," she said, "there are *five* fourth grade classes in my new school."

"That's nice," Mrs. Mace said. "You can be in a class that's just right for you."

Sometimes Jennifer wished her mother didn't have an answer for everything.

"I hate all the big buildings," she said.

"Prospect Park is near here," Mrs. Mace told her. "Why don't you walk over there and look at it?"

She just wants to get rid of me, said Jennifer to herself, but she put on her jacket and went out of the apartment. She didn't wait for the elevator. The Maces lived on the third floor. Jennifer ran down the stairs to the lobby.

When she was out on the street Jennifer looked around. A boy was delivering groceries to the apartment building. "Which way is the park?" she asked him.

He pointed down the street. "Just walk that way," he said. "You can't miss it."

Jennifer started walking past all the big apartment buildings. Here and there an old wooden house was sandwiched in between them. The old houses made Jennifer homesick for Carbondale.

At last she came to the park. It was much bigger than Jennifer had expected. There were roads running through it. Jennifer went through the gate and crossed a road to get to the bank of a large lake.

A duck with a shiny green head and neck was swimming offshore. Jennifer watched him dive down into the water until only his tail feathers stuck up in the air. After a minute the duck bobbed up again. He shook the water off his bill. Just as he was about to swim away a crust of bread sailed through the air and landed in the water near him. The duck gobbled the bread and looked to see if there was more where that came from.

Jennifer looked too. She saw an old man standing close to her on the bank of the lake.

That's funny, she thought. I didn't notice him before.

A fat pigeon sat on each of the old man's shoulders. Around his feet was a flock of starlings and sparrows. Jennifer couldn't be sure, but she thought she saw something peeping out of the side pocket of his baggy brown overcoat. The old man was throwing crumbs to the birds.

Suddenly there was a loud whirr of wings. All the birds flew up into the air and scattered. A huge black raven flew down and landed on the old man's floppy hat. "Oh hello, Napoleon. Where have you been?" The old man reached up to give the bird a piece of bread.

The raven stood on one foot and held the bread in the claws of the other. He cocked his head and kept a bright eye on Jennifer while he ate.

She took a step toward the bird, and the raven spread his wings and flapped away. "I must have scared him," Jennifer said. "I'm sorry."

The old man smiled down at her. His brown face was criss-crossed with wrinkles. It looked as dry and hard as the bark of an old tree. "Don't worry about Napoleon," he said. "He'll be back."

"Do you come here often to feed the birds?" Jennifer asked.

"They're my friends," the old man said. "I have to take care of them." He took a handful of nuts out of one of the many pockets of his coat. As if from nowhere a gray squirrel came running toward him. "See if you can get him to eat out of your hand." The old man gave Jennifer a little nut.

She stooped down and held it out to the squirrel. He put his head on one side. Jennifer made a chirping noise. The squirrel thought for a moment, took a good look at the nut, and slowly crept over to Jennifer. He sat up, holding his little paws in front of his chest.

"Don't be afraid," said Jennifer.

The squirrel made a quick grab for the nut, stuffed it in his mouth, and scampered up a beech tree. When he was halfway up the trunk of the tree he turned upside down. He clung there and watched Jennifer.

"I did it!" Jennifer turned to look at the bird man. She couldn't see him anywhere.

Jennifer looked again at the squirrel on the tree trunk. The tree was enormous. The tangled roots around the base were as big as the branches on ordinary trees. Jennifer saw a small hole in the trunk near the ground. She got down on her hands and knees and looked in. The tree seemed to be hollow inside.

I'm sure there's room enough in there for me, Jennifer told herself, but the hole is too small. The hole was too small even for her arm to reach in. She put her eye against it. There was a dim light inside the hole. Jennifer put her ear to it. She could hear faint fluttering sounds.

There must be a bird in there, she thought. But how did it get in? Maybe there's another hole at the top of the tree.

Jennifer stood a short distance away from the tree and looked up. Now she could see that the trunk of the tree had snapped off. It must have happened long ago. The branches had grown higher than the broken trunk.

A black shape flew out of the top of the tree trunk. It was the raven.

The squirrel had finished eating the nut. He swung himself right side up, climbed up into the tree, and disappeared behind a twisted old branch.

The sky over the apartment buildings across the street from the park was turning red. A cold November wind rustled the leaves on the walk by the lake. Jennifer turned up the collar of her jacket and dug her hands into her pockets. She went across the road to the gate of the park and walked home.

# 2

"HOW was the park, Jenny?" Mrs. Mace asked. She was paring apples to make a pie.

"I met a funny old man there," said Jennifer. "He was all covered with birds. He said they were his friends, and they didn't seem at all afraid of him." She went to get the rolling pin for her mother.

"I've seen people like that," her mother said. "They go to the same place every day. The birds wait for them."

"He gave me a nut, and a squirrel took it right out of my hand, Mother," Jennifer said. "Could you buy a bag of peanuts? Maybe I can make friends with the squirrel."

"Why don't you make friends with the children at school?" Mrs. Mace began to roll out her pie crust.

Jennifer chewed on a piece of apple peel. "Please, Mother," she said, "buy some peanuts."

"Oh, all right," Mrs. Mace said, "but promise you won't eat them in the house. I don't want peanut shells all over the place."

"I promise," said Jennifer.

Next day, when Jennifer came home from school, she found a bag of peanuts on the kitchen table. She remembered her promise to her mother. Instead of cracking a peanut, she spread a slice of bread with peanut butter and poured herself a glass of milk.

After she had finished her snack Jennifer put on her jacket, picked up the bag of peanuts, and went out.

She headed for the park. When she came to the gate she saw the big tree, but something about it looked different. Jennifer went over to it. The tree seemed to be in a different place from where it was yesterday. It was near a green park bench by the walk. The lower branches hung right over the bench.

It must be a new bench, Jennifer told herself. She looked at the concrete legs of the bench. They were weather-stained to the same color as the walk. The bench certainly didn't look new. She looked again at the tree. There was the little hole near the base. She looked up. The trunk was broken too. It was the same tree all right.

Now, where was the squirrel? Jennifer made her chirping noise. A little gray head poked around the big tree trunk. Jennifer pulled a peanut out of the bag. A hop at a time, the squirrel came over to her until he could grab the peanut. Then he jumped onto the back of the park bench to crack it. After he had eaten four peanuts, the squirrel dug a hole and buried the fifth one.

Jennifer heard a loud splash. She turned to look at the lake. A boy who was fishing had lost his footing and fallen into the water.

Jennifer ran to help. The water was not deep, but there were broken bottles and tin cans on the bottom of the lake. Jennifer kneeled down on the stone rim and held out her hand. The boy grabbed it and climbed out onto the shore.

"Are you hurt?" Jennifer asked.

"I'm all right," the boy said, "but my

fishing line is a mess." He was holding a small drop line. It was snarled around his shoes.

"Stand still," Jennifer said. "I think I can untangle it."

"I'd better take the hook off," the boy said. He bent down and untied the hook from the line.

Jennifer set to work pulling the string out of the loops it had made of itself. "What's your name?" she asked.

"Michael Stewart, but everybody calls me Mike," the boy told her. "What's yours?"

"Jennifer Mace." She untangled the last snarl and stood up.

Mike rolled up the fishing line. He squeezed the water out of the bottom of his pants legs and stamped his feet to try to get it out of his shoes.

"Can you really catch fish in the lake?" Jennifer asked.

"There aren't many now," Mike said. "In the beginning of the summer there were loads. Only people under sixteen are supposed to fish here, but lots of grown-ups do anyway. One Sunday I saw a woman with three fishing poles propped along the shore. I like the park better when there aren't so many people in it. Hardly anybody comes here when it's cold. What are you doing in the park?"

"I came here to feed the squirrels," Jennifer said. "Do you like peanuts?" She held out the bag.

"Do I!" Mike grinned. He reached into the bag.

Jennifer took a peanut too. For a while they munched away without talking. Then Mike said, "There's an old man who comes here to feed the birds and the squirrels."

"I know," Jennifer said. "That's how I got the idea." She turned to look for the squirrel. The old man was sitting on the park bench. There were birds all over him. "Look, Mike. There he is now." Jennifer waved to the bird man. He waved back.

Mike looked at the bird man. "Did you ever see so many birds, Jen? I wonder how he does it." He cracked another peanut.

"Let's go talk to him," Jennifer said. She walked over to the bench where the old man was sitting. Mike came after her. The birds flew away when the children came close to them. The old man moved over on the bench to make room. "Have a seat," he said.

Jennifer sat next to him, and Mike sat on the other side of her. "How do you make the birds so tame?" Mike asked.

The old man smiled. "They've known me a long time." He looked at Mike's soggy legs and feet. "What happened to you?"

"I fell in the lake," Mike said.

"It used to be a swamp," the bird man said. "People were always falling into it then."

"What was the park like in those days?" Jennifer asked.

"It was a dark tangled wood, with little secret paths and heavy underbrush. All kinds of birds and animals lived here then."

Mike interrupted. "That's not what my father told me. He said it used to be very grand, with Greek temples and rose gardens and none of the trash there is nowadays."

"That was later," the bird man said. "Fine ladies drove through the park in open carriages in summer, and in the winter people skated on the lake."

"They don't allow skating on the lake now," Mike said. "You have to go to the ice skating rink." He looked down at his wet shoes. "I'm beginning to feel icy my-

self. I'd better go home." He stood up.
"Which way is your house, Jen?"

"I live on Ocean Parkway." Jennifer got
to her feet.

The children said good-by to the bird
man and walked across the road. At the
gate of the park Jennifer turned to look
back. She couldn't see the old man anywhere. The big tree stood on the other
side of the walk from the park bench.

# 3

JENNIFER and Mike walked down
Ocean Parkway eating peanuts. "Mike,"
said Jennifer when she had finished four,
"there's a big tree in the park that moves
around."

Mike gave her a funny look. "You mean
it grows in one place one day and in another the next?"

"Yes," Jennifer said, "and sometimes it
isn't there at all."

Mike nodded. "I noticed the same thing,
but I never told anybody. They'd only say

I was crazy. It's a hollow tree, Jen. I'd climb into it, but I'm afraid it might disappear with me in it."

"There must be some way to do it," Jennifer said. "It doesn't disappear while you're looking at it. If one of us climbed in while the other one kept an eye on the tree — "

Mike looked at her with admiration. "I never thought of that," he said. When they came to the next corner he pointed to an old frame house on the side street. "That's where I live."

Jennifer showed him the big apartment building halfway down the next block. "We're in apartment C on the third floor," she said. "Do you go to my school? I'm in Mrs. Gilpin's class."

"That's 4-1," said Mike. "I'm in 4-4, two rooms down the hall from you." He took another peanut and then turned the corner. "Bye. See you in school."

Jennifer's mother met her when she walked into the apartment. "I see you found the peanuts, Jenny. Did the squirrel like them?"

"Yes, but I ate more than he did." Jennifer followed her mother into the kitchen. She put the nearly empty bag of peanuts on the table.

"I hope you're not too full to eat supper," Mrs. Mace said.

"I had help eating the peanuts." Jennifer told her mother about meeting Mike. She didn't tell her about the tree.

Next day Mike waited for Jennifer in the school yard and walked home with her. "I'll take my books home and get some clothesline," he said. "And I'd better put on some old pants. Meet me in front of your building."

There was no sunshine that afternoon, and the wind was bitterly cold. Jennifer changed into flannel-lined jeans and put a sweater under her jacket. Mike was waiting for her when she came downstairs. The front of his jacket was bulging.

"Did you get the clothesline?" Jennifer asked.

"Yes. I had to hide it from my grandmother. She watches everything I do." Mike pulled a coil of rope out of his jacket. "My mother's too busy to give me any trouble, but Grandma doesn't seem to have anything else to do." He looped the clothesline over his arm.

On the way to the park they decided that Jennifer should keep her eyes on the tree while Mike climbed up to the hole and lowered himself into it by the rope. Then Mike would take a turn at watching while Jennifer climbed.

The bird man was sitting on the bench by the walk. The big black raven was perched on his shoulder and seemed to be talking to him. The bird man was so interested in what the raven was saying that he didn't notice Jennifer and Mike. The big tree was nowhere in sight.

"Wouldn't you just know we couldn't find it today?" Mike dug his fists into his pockets and kicked at a clump of dry grass.

"Do you think we ought to look for it somewhere else in the park?" Jennifer asked.

"Don't you know how big the park is, Jen?" Mike said. "There are hundreds of trees in it."

"I never saw the park until a couple of days ago," Jennifer explained. "We just moved here."

"Well," Mike said, "since we're here, we ought to be able to find something else to do." He walked down to the shore of the big lake.

Over to the right was a small wooded

island. It was not far from the shore. A large branch had fallen from a tree on the mainland. It stretched across the water toward the island.

"Hey, Jen, look at that!" Mike was excited. "We could use that for a bridge. I've always wanted to explore the island." He ran along the bank and scrambled out onto the fallen branch.

Mike crawled along the branch. Jennifer stood on the shore and watched. Mike made a lasso out of the clothesline and tossed it over a bush on the island. He held onto the rope to steady himself as he moved to the island shore.

"Your turn now, Jen." Mike threw the end of the clothesline to Jennifer. It took her by surprise. She almost missed catching it, but she made a lucky grab and took hold of the rope. She felt like a tight-rope walker as she put one foot in front of the other and balanced her way along the branch.

When she reached the shore Mike was already pushing through the stiff yellow weeds and grass that grew on the island. It was taller than the grass on the mainland. They couldn't see over it.

Jennifer kept right behind Mike and followed the path he made. A cold wind rattled the grass around them.

# 4

THEY had been walking for quite a while. "We ought to come to the other side of the island soon," Mike said. He went on pushing through the tangle of weeds.

Jennifer noticed that they were going downhill. The grass was taller than ever. Little by little it seemed to come together over their heads until at last they were walking through a grassy tunnel. At first the light that came through the grass was pale gold, but as they went along it changed to a soft green.

Mike stopped and looked around. The grass in front was thinner now. There were strange curling branches growing down from the roof of the tunnel. He saw a little animal asleep on one of the twisting branches. "What do you suppose this is, Jen?"

Jennifer stood on tiptoe to get a better look. "What soft fur it has! It looks just like velvet." She reached up to touch the animal. It squirmed in its sleep and stretched out a pointed snout. "Oh, Mike," Jennifer said, "it's a mole."

"I never saw one before," said Mike. "I thought they lived underground. Are you sure that's what it is?"

"Yes," Jennifer said. "Last summer Dad dug one out of our lawn in Carbondale."

Now they both noticed that there were many creatures in the forest above them. Most of them were little wormy things. Some of them glowed in the shadowy

clumps of the trees. They could hear the sound of water gurgling all around them, but they couldn't see a stream anywhere.

"Jen," Mike said in a whisper, "it isn't cold any more! There's something funny about all this."

The air around them was warm and damp. There was no wind at all. The branches above them were laced together, but Jennifer began to see that they belonged to different trees. A network of little thread-like twigs fanned out in all directions.

There were no leaves on the branches, and it looked as if there never had been any. All around was the strange green glow. It seemed to move with the children as they walked.

"I never thought the island was like this," Mike said.

Jennifer bent back a long trailing branch. "I don't think we're on the island any longer, Mike," she said slowly. "I think we're *under* it."

Mike stared hard at the trees growing upside down. "You're right, Jen," he said. "They're not branches at all. They're *roots*."

"Somehow we've gone under the ground," Jennifer said, "and the dirt has just turned to air. Those little round things up there look like acorns sprouting."

"Everything was so cold and dead up on top," Mike said. "Here it's all so alive."

They could almost see the roots growing in the warm stillness. Mike and Jennifer went from one clump to another until they came to an enormous tree. Thick branch-like roots twisted all around it. Jennifer sat down on one of them and swung her legs back and forth. High overhead in the roots she saw a nest of sleeping mice. Above them a little hole shone with a different light.

Mike saw the hole too. "That's daylight, Jen," he said, "but the hole is too small for us to get out by. We'd better go back the way we came."

Jennifer slipped off the big root, ready to follow Mike. He turned around. The tunnel they had come through was no longer there. A thick jungle of tree roots surrounded them.

"Now what?" Mike asked.

Only a minute before Jennifer was happy to be in the warm green underground world. Now it looked as if she and Mike were trapped here. Suddenly everything seemed different. The soft green light was scary.

Jennifer looked up at the white light coming from the mouse hole high above them. "Let's dig our way out," she said. She began to climb the upside-down tree, grabbing hold of the roots and forcing her way up.

Mike coughed. "I can hardly breathe. There seems to be more dirt than air." He was scrambling up the network of roots toward the mouse hole. As he went he pushed the dirt aside with his hands and squirmed through it.

Jennifer reached the hole first. She turned her finger like a screw in it. The hole became a little bigger. Jennifer could shove her arm through it now. She couldn't turn her head to see Mike. Now and then he tapped her foot to let her know he was right behind her.

The dirt was harder now — and colder. Jennifer could hardly get through it. She twisted her whole body and fought her way up through the dirt. Spluttering and choking, she pulled herself through the hole into the cold, wintry air. Huge lumpy tree roots were all around her. Jennifer grabbed hold of them to climb out of the ground.

She stood up and shook the dirt off herself like a dog shaking off water after a swim. Then she kneeled down to grab Mike's hand which was just poking out of the hole.

A moment later Mike too was in the open, stamping his feet and shaking himself. He looked up. "Hey, Jen, this is the magic tree!"

## 5

THEY were standing near the park bench.

"We must have walked in a circle and gone back under the lake," Mike said. "Well, at least we've found the tree. Hand me the rope."

"I don't have it, Mike," Jennifer said. "It's still tied to the bush on the shore of the island."

"Caw, caw, caw!" The raven was sitting in one of the top branches of the tree.

Jennifer thought he was laughing at them.

Mike frowned. "Keep your eyes on the tree, Jen," he said. "I'll get the rope." He ran back along the rim of the lake to where the broken tree branch made a bridge to the island. Jennifer sat on the bench and stared at the magic tree.

It seemed an age before Mike came back. When he did he was soaking wet and shivering, but he had the clothesline. "I fell in," he explained.

"It's getting dark," Jennifer said, "and you'd better get out of those wet clothes. We'll have to climb the tree another time."

They went out of the park and walked quickly homeward.

"I don't really feel much like climbing now," Mike admitted. "I was tired after all that digging to get out of the ground. Falling in the lake just finished the job." He grinned. "Now I have to think of some-

thing to tell Grandma when she sees me
like this."

Jennifer laughed. If Mike told his
grandmother everything that had happened to him she'd think he was lying. "Just
tell her you fell in the lake."

"She might tell me I can't go near the
park again. And she's going to be mad
about the wet clothesline," Mike said.

Jennifer thought hard for a minute.

"There's a laundromat in the basement of our apartment building," she said. "You could put your clothes and the clothesline in the dryer there. I have a dime."

"What would I wear in the meantime?" Mike asked.

Jennifer thought again. "Come up to my apartment," she said.

Mrs. Mace was setting the table for supper when they walked in. "You're late, Jenny," she said.

"I'm sorry, Mother," said Jennifer. "This is Mike. He fell in the lake again. I want to dry his clothes so he doesn't have to go home wet."

"Hello, Mike," Mrs. Mace said. She got out a raincoat for him to wear while Jennifer took his clothes to the basement. "Were you fishing again?" she asked.

"No," Mike said. "I was using a tree branch for a bridge to the island, and I slipped."

"Is the water deep?" Mrs. Mace looked worried.

"No," said Mike.

"Then you can go wading in the summertime," Jennifer's mother said.

Mike didn't tell her about the cans and broken bottles on the bottom of the lake. He was glad when Mrs. Mace went back into the kitchen. Jennifer's father came home soon after. He said hello to Mike and then sat down to read his newspaper.

Mike pulled the raincoat around himself and sat on the edge of the sofa. He counted the minutes until Jennifer came back. He knew he would be in trouble if he came home late — perhaps more than if he had come home wet.

When Jennifer returned, Mike quickly changed back into his clothes. They were still a little damp. It was dark outside and colder than ever. He ran all the way home.

His mother was waiting for him. "Your

dad is working late," she said. "It's a good thing we're having stew tonight. It doesn't spoil waiting."

"Where's Grandma?" Mike asked.

"Oh, she had an early dinner and went to the movies."

# 6

THE next day was Saturday. Right after breakfast Mike came to call for Jennifer. He was wearing a thick quilted jacket and had a cap pulled down over his ears.

"You look as if you're going to the North Pole," Jennifer told him.

"The forecast is for snow," Mrs. Mace said. "Wear your mittens, Jenny."

When they reached the park the first few flakes were drifting down. They caught on Jennifer's eyelashes. The big tree was right beside the bench, just where they had left it yesterday. There was the hole between the roots through which they had crawled out of the ground. It was now only big enough for a mouse.

"I'm going to climb the tree before it gets away again." Mike pulled the clothesline out from under his jacket.

Jennifer looked up at the tree. The break in the trunk was very high up. "It's snowing, Mike," she said. "You might slip."

Mike wasn't listening. He had grabbed the lowest branch of the big beech tree and swung himself up onto it. Jennifer stood under the tree and watched him climb. It was snowing harder now. The soft flakes fell on her upturned face.

When Mike had climbed to the place where the trunk had broken off, he looked down into the hole. "It's awfully dark in there," he said.

"Maybe you shouldn't go into it," said Jennifer.

"I might never get another chance."

Mike began to tie the clothesline around a branch.

Suppose the tree disappears with Mike in it, Jennifer thought, even though I have my eyes on it? Or suppose something makes me look away for a second? "Mike!" she called. "Don't do it! Come on back down!"

Mike paid no attention to her. He was busy fastening the rope around his waist. A moment later he had slipped into the hole at the top of the tree, and Jennifer couldn't see him any more. She couldn't even hear him as he went down inside the trunk.

She put her mouth to the hole in the trunk near the base of the tree. "Mike, are you all right?" Then Jennifer put her ear to the little hole. She heard a fluttering noise from inside the tree. "Mike!" she called. There was no answer.

Jennifer didn't waste any more time.

She started to climb the tree. The branches were not too far apart. Jennifer went higher and higher. The snowflakes whirled around her. She stopped to look down. It made her dizzy. Jennifer decided not to do that again. When at last she reached the branch where Mike had tied the clothesline she grabbed the rope and pulled.

It came up easily into her hand. At the end was the big loop that had gone around Mike's waist, but the loop was empty.

Jennifer leaned over the black hole in the tree. "Mike!" she called down into the darkness.

This time there was a cooing sound from below.

Jennifer slipped the looped end of the rope over her head and arms. She tightened it around her waist. Then, slowly, holding onto the rope, she lowered herself into the hole.

At first Jennifer braced herself against the inside of the tree trunk to slow her descent, but soon it became impossible. She just couldn't reach the trunk any more. Then the rope around her waist became loose. Jennifer tried to tighten it, but her fingers fluttered in a feathery way and couldn't grab the rope. It slipped away from her.

Jennifer expected to fall. She waved her arms wildly. To her surprise she found herself rising in the air. *I'm flying*, Jennifer thought.

She lowered her arms and coasted slowly down. Now she saw an opening like a round window. It was the hole in the lower part of the tree. But it seemed so much bigger than Jennifer remembered!

"Coo!" There was that noise again, but this time it seemed like words. It sounded like Mike's voice. "Jen," it seemed to say, "is that you?"

Jennifer's eyes were getting used to the darkness. The light from the little window was just enough for her to see a small brown pigeon standing on a pile of old leaves and rotting twigs at the bottom of the hollow tree. The pigeon opened its beak and said again, "Jen?"

"Oh, Mike, what's happened to you?" Jennifer fluttered down beside the bird.

"Looking at you," the bird said, "I begin to understand. We've both turned into pigeons."

Jennifer looked down at her feet. "I'm certainly pigeon-toed," she said.

At this Mike laughed so hard that he fluttered right up off the ground. "Hey, this is great," he said. "I can fly. I was wondering how I was going to get out of here without the rope. I called to you, but you didn't seem to hear me. It shouldn't be hard to get out with wings." Mike flapped and turned, practicing flying. Then, like a helicopter, he rose slowly upward, flying in a spiral. "Follow me," he cooed as he burst forth from the top of the tree trunk.

Jennifer fluttered after him.

# 7

MIKE flew through the falling snow toward a high hill. The cold air swished past his wings as he swooped over the treetops.

Jennifer had always wanted to fly. Her whole body tingled with the exercise, and she didn't feel the least bit cold. When Mike flew down to perch on the branch of a sycamore tree she fluttered down beside him.

Jennifer's eyes shone. "I want to fly around the whole park, Mike," she said. "I've never seen all of it."

Mike fluffed out the feathers on his neck and shook himself. "The zoo is on the other side of the park," he said. "Have you ever been there?"

Jennifer shook her head.

"Then what are we waiting for?" Mike jumped into the air and soared high over the trees. "We can take a short cut over the lake," he called back over his shoulder. He curved around and flew down from the hill.

Jennifer looked back. Right at the top of the hill was a circular walk and a row of old lamp posts. It looks like a good place for a picnic, she thought. Mike was already starting to fly over the lake. Jennifer hurried to catch up with him. The snow was falling so thickly now that soon she couldn't see the little pigeon flying ahead of her.

She flew faster, but still there was no sign of Mike. Jennifer had crossed the lake and gone over a strip of trees. There were houses below. Jennifer had flown right out of the park. She was lost.

She turned around and flew in what she thought was the direction she had come. It was no use. All she came to were houses and more houses. Jennifer was getting tired. She flew down and rested on the windowsill of a large apartment building. She fluffed up her feathers and huddled against the glass.

Suddenly the window opened. A hand grabbed Jennifer. She looked up into the face of a boy. "Ma!" he yelled, "look what I caught!"

The door of the room opened, and a fat woman came in. When she saw Jennifer she smiled. "Squab!" she said. "I'll stuff it with sausage meat. Where'd you get it, Steve?"

"On the windowsill. The stupid thing was just sitting there waiting for me to catch it."

I'll show you who's stupid, said Jennifer to herself. She closed her eyes, held her breath, and stayed very still.

"Steve," the woman said, "there's something the matter with this bird."

"It was all right a minute ago," the boy said, looking hard at Jennifer. He put her down on the table.

Jennifer lay on her back and let her legs stick stiffly up in the air. Steve prodded her with his finger. Even though it tickled, Jennifer didn't stir a feather.

"It must have been sick," the fat woman said. She sounded disappointed. "You'd better throw it away. Take it out to the incinerator."

Steve picked Jennifer up by one wing feather and carried her into the hall. She opened her eyes and saw that the elevator had stopped at that floor. A man was getting out. Jennifer curved her neck and gave Steve a sharp peck on the hand.

"Ow!" He let go of her.

Jennifer twisted in mid-air, beat her wings rapidly, and flew into the elevator. She pecked hard at the first floor button. The elevator door closed, and the elevator started down.

It passed two floors. Then it stopped. A man and a woman stepped into the elevator. Jennifer hid in the corner behind the fan.

When the elevator stopped on the main floor everybody got out. Jennifer flew into the lobby. The woman who had been in the elevator saw her. "Shoo!" she said, and held the front door open so that the pigeon could fly out.

Jennifer was happy to be outdoors again. It had stopped snowing. She took a deep breath and flew very high over the apartment building. To the left she saw the big park. Jennifer decided to fly around the edge of it. It wasn't the shortest route, but that way she was sure to come to the zoo.

Now that the sun was shining Jennifer had no trouble finding the zoo. She spotted it first by an orange balloon that had escaped from somebody and was floating up into the blue sky. Jennifer flew down and through the main gate. She perched on the iron railing by the sea lions and looked for Mike.

# 8

A FLOCK of pigeons was eating crack-erjacks off the pavement. Jennifer flew over to join them. A large pigeon with a beautiful green and purple neck glared at her with angry red eyes. "Go find your own dinner," he said.

"I don't want your food," Jennifer said. "I'm looking for someone. Have you seen a small brown pigeon anywhere around here?"

"You mean you're not the one I chased before?" said the pigeon. "He ate three crackerjacks before I could stop him."

"That sounds like Mike." Jennifer cocked her head. She stretched her wings. "Which way did he go?"

The big pigeon jerked his neck in the direction of a walk that was lined with cages. Jennifer flew over there. She fluttered from cage to cage, looking in all of them.

At the end of the row of cages Jennifer crossed another walk. She came to a high fence in front of a ditch full of water. On the other side of the ditch was a rocky hill with caves in it.

A crowd of people stood in front of the fence. They were pushing to see past each other. A little girl in the crowd screamed. Jennifer heard a man say, "The bird will do that once too often!"

Jennifer flew to the top of a lamp post.

From here she could see over the heads of the people.

Two boys were standing just outside the bars of the cage. A large black bear was on the other side of the ditch. He sat up and raised his paws in the air. One of the boys threw a peanut to him. It bounced off a rock.

Just as the bear grabbed for the peanut, a bird swooped down and snatched it. Then he flew up onto a big rock over the bear's cave. He perched there to crack open the peanut. The bear snarled. He jumped as high as he could but he couldn't reach the bird. The bird ate the nut and tossed the empty shell to the bear.

Some of the people thought this was very funny. Jennifer didn't. The bird was a pigeon, a little brown one.

The boy at the fence waited until the pigeon had eaten the nut. Then he threw another one into the cage. This time the bird caught the peanut before it hit the ground. Again he flew onto the rocks to eat it. The black bear growled. His red tongue was hanging out of his mouth.

Jennifer flew over the bars of the cage to where the pigeon was crunching away. She perched on the rock beside him. "Stop it, Mike! You know it's wrong to tease animals."

He tipped his head on one side and looked at her with a shining eye. "Great peanuts," he said.

"You don't have any right to them," Jennifer said.

"They're better than stale crackerjacks, and I was hungry. What took you so long, Jen?" Mike had eaten half the peanut. He dropped the other half down to the bear.

"I lost sight of you in the falling snow over the lake. I nearly was eaten." Jennifer told Mike about her adventure.

"That Steve sounds like a rotten kid,"

Mike said. "I'd like to get even with him."

"I wonder what time it is," Jennifer said. "I ought to go home for lunch. My mother will be waiting for me."

"So will mine. I guess we'd better go back." Mike jumped into the air and flew out of the bear's cage. Jennifer hurried after him. She didn't want to get lost again.

They were flying over an open grassy space in the park. "That's called the Long Meadow," Mike told Jennifer.

She was very quiet. She remembered now that her mother didn't like pigeons very much. "Mike," she said, "suppose my mother doesn't let me in? It's fun to be a bird, but I'm not sure I want to be one always."

They flew along in silence. As they passed over the walk near the lake Jennifer looked down and saw the big tree.

"It's still there, Mike," she said. "Maybe if we fly into it again we'll change back."

"It's worth a try." Mike fluttered down and perched on the branch to which he had tied the clothesline. He looked at the rope and scratched his head with one claw. "Jen," he said, "the clothesline isn't nearly long enough to get to the bottom of the tree. If we change back when we're down there we'll never get out."

"Serves you right," a harsh voice said. "You never should have gone into the tree in the first place."

Mike and Jennifer both turned to see where the voice had come from. They couldn't see anyone.

"A big nuisance this thing is," the voice went on. "It gets in my way whenever I want to go in or out."

The voice seemed to come from inside the tree. Jennifer flew over the hole in the top of the trunk and looked down. She saw the raven Napoleon slowly climbing the rope. He reached the top of the hole and stepped off the rope onto the broken trunk. "Didn't anyone ever teach you two not to go into people's homes without an invitation?"

"Oh," Jennifer said, "are you a person too?"

Napoleon glared at her. "What do you mean? Of course, I'm a person! But if you

mean am I a stupid human like you, no.
I wouldn't want to be."

"We're not either stupid," said Mike.
"I'm sorry the rope is in your way. If I
were changed back to myself I'd take it
out of the tree, but it's too heavy for me
now."

The raven looked at him sideways. "If
I tell you how to get back to your own
ugly shape will you promise, both of you,
never to go into the tree again?"

"Yes," Mike said.

Napoleon turned to Jennifer. "What about you?"

"I promise," she said.

"All right then." Napoleon hopped onto the branch beside Mike. "See if you can find a beech nut on the tree."

The two little pigeons began to search among the bare branches. At last Mike found a nut. He pulled it off the tree with his beak and flew down to the sidewalk with it.

"Divide it between you," the raven ordered.

Jennifer flew down beside Mike. She watched while he tore off the outer shell of the beech nut. Two little nuts fell onto the pavement.

"Eat them!" Napoleon commanded.

Jennifer pecked away at one of the little three-cornered nuts. She ate half of it, but still there was no change in her shape or size. "It's not working," Jennifer said. She looked up sadly.

There was Mike in his thick jacket with the hat pulled down over his ears. "Eat the rest, Jen," he told her.

Jennifer set to work to finish the nut. As soon as she had eaten it she discovered that she was down on her hands and knees with her nose against the pavement. She got to her feet and looked around. The tree was gone.

The bird man was sitting on the park bench.

## 9

THE days were getting shorter. There wasn't much time after school before it was dark. On week ends Jennifer and Mike took long walks in the park. Once they found an old cemetery on the top of a hill. It was fenced with chicken wire that had barbed wire on top.

"It's a funny place for a graveyard," Jennifer said. "I wonder why it's here."

She followed Mike along a path that ran beside the fence. They cut through some woods and then went down a slope toward the lake. The bird man was standing near a monument on the side of the hill. As usual he was surrounded by birds.

"Hello," he said when he saw Jennifer and Mike. The birds didn't fly away this time when the children came over to the old man. "Either they're getting used to you or they're too hungry to worry about you," he said.

Jennifer wondered if somehow she and Mike seemed different to the birds since they had been birds themselves. The birds seemed different to her now. For one thing she could still understand what they were saying. When a quick little sparrow snatched a crumb from under the beak of a pigeon she heard the pigeon say, "Do that again and you'll lose a tail feather."

"There's enough for everybody," the

bird man said. "You know I don't like quarreling."

Mike was looking at the monument, a marble column with a fence around it. "The Maryland Brigade," he read. "I wonder who they were."

"Youngsters," the old man said. "Most of them were still in their teens."

"What's the monument for?" Mike asked.

The old man looked sad. "They were fighting a battle," he said, "surrounded by an army much bigger than theirs. The older soldiers who knew they didn't stand a chance ran away. The Maryland boys stayed to fight. It gave the others time to escape. Most of the Marylanders are buried on the hill over there."

Mike and Jennifer were silent for a minute. Jennifer wondered when all this had happened. The bird man sounded as if he knew the boys who died. She looked at the monument. August 27, 1776, it said.

Why that's the American revolution, Jennifer thought. The old man couldn't be old enough to remember that.

There was a scream from overhead. Jennifer looked up. A gray sea gull sailed down over the treetops and landed neatly on the water. Jennifer saw that there was ice around the edge of the lake. The gull joined a flock of others who were swimming in the middle.

"Why are there *sea* gulls on the lake?" Jennifer wanted to know.

"It's more sheltered here than by the ocean," the bird man said.

Each time Mike and Jennifer came back to the park they saw more gulls on the lake. When the lake was almost all frozen the gulls walked about on the ice. There seemed to be thousands of them.

In the part of the lake that wasn't frozen there were big white ducks. Jennifer thought they might have escaped from a farmyard. She saw funny little black grebes too. They bobbed their heads up and down when they swam. The ducks with the beautiful green necks were still on the lake, and one day Mike spotted a gray goose walking along the shore.

The raven Napoleon was often in the trees overhanging the lake, but he never went in the water.

The bird man was in the park every time they went there. On the coldest days, when they had to run to keep warm, they

saw him standing, throwing crumbs to the pigeons and sparrows or sitting on the bench with the raven on his shoulder. Sometimes there was snow on his hat, but he never bothered to brush it off.

The ground was frozen. It crunched under their feet. Snow had covered the ice on the lake as well as the hills around it. "We could walk to the island," Mike said.

"Didn't you see the sign, Mike?" Jennifer pointed to it.

DANGER
KEEP OFF THE ICE

"I'd like to get over to the island," Mike said. "I wish I had the clothesline, but it's in the tree. And we never see the tree any more."

"Caw, caw, caw!" The raven Napoleon croaked at them from a branch overhead.

## 10

ONE Saturday afternoon Mike put his foot through the ice on the lake. Jennifer went home with him. She sat down in the living room while Mike went upstairs to change his shoes.

Jennifer heard the front door open. A moment later a little old woman came into the house, stamping her feet to get the snow off her boots. She took off her mittens and was just about to take off her hat when she saw Jennifer.

Jennifer stood up. "I'm Jennifer Mace," she said.

The old woman looked at her with bright dark eyes. "Oh, you're the lass who fished Mike out of the lake." She held out her hand. "How do you do? I'm Mike's grandmother, Mrs. Craig."

Jennifer shook Mrs. Craig's hand.

Mike's grandmother took off her hat and coat and scarf and put them away in the hall closet. She came back into the living room. "I suppose Mike fell into the lake

again today," she said. "He'll be changing his shoes now."

"However did you know?" Jennifer asked.

"That boy *always* falls in the lake," his grandmother said. "I understand you're a newcomer here, Jennifer. How do you like Brooklyn?"

"I like it better now than I did at first," Jennifer said. "It's dirty and crowded, but I'm getting used to it."

Mrs. Craig nodded her head. "I know just how you feel. When I first came here I wasn't any older than you are, and I hated the place. I missed the little town in Scotland where I used to live. I didn't know anybody here. The first friend I made was an old man in the park. He came there to feed the birds." Mrs. Craig sighed. "The park was beautiful in those days."

"It still is," Jennifer said. "And Mike and I know a man there who feeds the birds too. We call him the bird man."

Mike came to the head of the stairs and looked over. "Hi, Grandma," he called down. "How was the movie? This is Jennifer."

"Jennifer and I have met," his grandmother said. "She's very nice, which is more than I can say for that dreadful movie."

Mike raced down the stairs. "Come on, Jen. Let's go back to the park."

His grandmother looked at his shoes. "Put your rubbers on, Mike," she said.

Mike dived into the hall closet. He began to look for his rubbers among the clutter of umbrellas and overshoes on the floor. Jennifer found them for him. They were wedged in a corner behind the vacuum cleaner.

Jennifer got back into her jacket and pulled on her knitted cap. "It's snowing again," she said, taking a look out of the window. "If I were back home in Carbondale I'd go sledding."

Mike grinned. "Wait for me on the porch. I have to get something."

Jennifer went out onto the front porch. She leaned against the wooden railing and watched the fat white flakes drifting down. They frosted the rooftops and covered the bits of trash that always littered the pavement. Snow clung to the bare branches of the trees along the street.

Everything was just beginning to look like a Christmas card when the front door opened and Mike came bumping out. He was carrying a long sled.

"It's pretty dusty," he said. "Somebody stuck it behind the furnace in the cellar. I'll go get some rags so we can clean it up." He went back into the house.

Jennifer was looking at the sled when she heard the front door open again.

"Here, rub this on the runners. It'll make it go faster." Mike's grandmother handed her a leftover piece of soap. She ducked back into the house before Jennifer could thank her.

After they dusted the sled, Mike towed it to the park. They joined a group of children who were sliding down a hill. Jennifer had never seen so many there before. Some of the children had sleds, but others were sliding on pieces of cardboard or plastic dish-like things. One boy was using the lid of a garbage can. He slid down the hill faster than anybody else.

They were having so much fun in the snow that it wasn't until they were ready to leave that Jennifer noticed the big old tree standing on the bank of the lake. The raven was sitting on one of the top branches.

"Look, Mike," said Jennifer.

Mike looked at the tree. The snow was thick on the gnarled old branches. "I can't see the rope from here," he said. "Do you think somebody took it?"

"It's beginning to get dark, Mike," Jennifer said. "You'd better get the rope another time."

"Caw, caw, caw!" called Napoleon from the top of the tree.

"Did you hear that, Jen?" Mike whispered. "It sounded just like words to me!"

"Yes," Jennifer said. "Didn't you know we still can understand bird talk? He said he doesn't want you to take the rope out of the tree."

"Why not, Napoleon?" Mike shouted.

He heard the bird answer, "It's been here so long I've gotten used to it. I can do my exercises on it in the morning without anybody making nasty remarks."

"Don't you get enough exercise just flying around?" Jennifer asked.

"I'm not as young as I used to be," Napoleon said.

"It's my mother's clothesline, and she keeps asking me where it is," Mike argued.

"Oh, let Napoleon have it, Mike. You can't climb the tree now. It's coated with ice. Anyway it's almost dark. I'm supposed to be home before the street lights go on." Jennifer tugged at his arm.

"O.K., Napoleon," Mike said. "You can keep it for now." He turned away from the tree. "Hey, Jen, what about taking turns towing each other home on the sled?"

## 11

THE week after Christmas was extremely cold. Mike decided that the ice on the lake was hard enough to walk on. "I want to go back to the island," he said.

Jennifer threw a rock onto the ice. It bounced on the hard surface and didn't even scratch it. "What are we going to do on the island?" she asked.

"I don't know," Mike said, "but the ice isn't often this thick. If we don't go now we may never get another chance."

"All right, Mike," Jennifer said, "but be careful." She stepped onto the frozen lake and walked across to the island. The fallen tree branch was sticking up out of the ice. Jennifer stayed close to it. "We want to be sure we go the same way we went before," she said.

Mike was right behind her. At the shore of the island they stopped. The tall grass was half buried in snowdrifts. Mike pushed his way into it, but it was frozen hard, and the going was difficult. Jennifer followed in his steps.

Suddenly a flock of wild ducks flew out of the grass. They quacked insults at the two children. "I wish I couldn't understand them," Jennifer said. "I don't like being called a stupid plucked chicken."

"Don't pay any attention, Jen," Mike

said. "We ought to be coming to the tunnel soon."

"Caw, caw, caw!" Now it was the raven flying over them. Napoleon seemed very excited. He beat his wings in an effort to stay in one place and flew in little circles around Jennifer and Mike.

Jennifer stopped walking and grabbed Mike by the sleeve to stop him too. "What's the matter, Napoleon?"

"The ground is frozen," cawed the bird, out of the breath from his efforts to stay close to them. "If you do get under it you'll never get out. You can't live without food till spring any more than I can."

Mike took another step forward. Jennifer tried to pull him back. She slipped and fell, pulling Mike down with her. The grass seemed to close over their heads. Jennifer felt as if she were being smothered. "Mike!" she gasped. "We have to get out of here!"

"I can't see," Mike said. "It's gotten dark."

They were lying in a tangled heap. The grass twisted around them, tying them down. It was freezing into a hard cage.

"Which way did we come?" Mike asked. "I'm so turned around I can't tell."

Jennifer had an idea. "Napoleon!" she screamed. "Which is the way out?"

She heard a faint cawing. "Stand up. The grass isn't so tough at the top."

Jennifer struggled to her feet. She pushed with her shoulders against the roof of grass. There was a cracking noise. Mike began to break the blades of grass like straws.

After what seemed an age the children made a small hole in the tough thatch above them. They had to work fast. The grass seemed to push together almost as fast as they could tear it apart.

At last Mike managed to shove his arm through the hole. The broken stems of grass tore at his sleeve. Then something sharp snapped at his hand. "Ouch!" Mike flailed his arm wildly and tried to hit the thing. It gave a loud cry.

"Idiot!" he heard the raven caw.

Mike tore his way into the open. "What did you say, Napoleon?"

The raven was perched on the branch of a tree. "I wasn't talking to you. This fat-headed sea bird thought you were some kind of fish."

Mike saw a hungry-looking gull hovering overhead. "Do your fishing somewhere else," Mike told him. He turned to give Jennifer a hand as she climbed out of the hole.

"Why don't you stay where you belong?" screamed the sea gull. "Then nobody could make a mistake." He flew off across the lake to join the other gulls who were walking about on the ice.

Jennifer looked down at the ground. "Mike," she said, "the hole has disappeared."

They were standing on a mat of frozen crushed grass. There was no sign of an opening in it. Neither Mike nor Jennifer wanted to stay any longer on the island. As quickly as they could they made their way to the shore and started back to the mainland.

The raven stayed where he was on the tree branch. He seemed to be watching to see that they got across the ice safely.

## 12

THE March days were still very cold, but Jennifer saw that the buds on the tree branches were swelling. She and Mike were talking to the bird man while he tossed crumbs to the birds. Jennifer thought there was something different about him.

The old man pulled something out of his pocket and threw it to a bird who had just fluttered down onto the walk. "Hello," he said, "glad to see you back."

"It's a robin!" Jennifer said. "That means spring is almost here."

"Yes," the bird man answered with a smile.

Suddenly Jennifer knew what was different about him. His brown hat and coat were faintly tinged with green!

"Spring!" Mike said. "We'll be able to go bike-riding."

"I don't have a bicycle any more," Jennifer told him. "I used to have one when we lived in Carbondale, but I got too big for it. We gave it to my cousin when we moved."

"You could ride on my handlebars," Mike said.

Jennifer shook her head. "I'm not allowed to ride double," she said. "My mother says it isn't safe."

"We'll take turns on mine then," said Mike. He looked disappointed.

When Jennifer got home she told her

mother, "There are special bicycle paths in the park, and on Saturday and Sunday the roads are closed to cars. I'm sure it would be safe for Mike and me to ride two on a bike."

Mrs. Mace was patching the knees on a pair of Jennifer's blue jeans. "I'll talk to Daddy about it when he comes home, Jenny," she said. "How is your friend, the old man who feeds the birds?"

"It's a funny thing, Mother," Jennifer said. "His brown coat and hat are turning green."

Her mother stuck her finger with the needle. She frowned and sucked the finger. Then she said, "Clothes do look a kind of dull moldy green when they're very old."

Now that the days were getting longer, there was time to go to the park after school. The bird man was always there, feeding the squirrels and the birds. His hat and coat were getting greener every day — not a dull moldy green at all but bright fresh green.

Little red leaves popped out on the bushes by the lake. The ice had nearly all melted. Jennifer saw a woodpecker and a yellow-shafted flicker. Mike pointed out that there were fewer sea gulls on the lake. "I'll be glad to see the last of them," he said.

The raven was often with the old man near the park bench, but the big tree was nowhere to be seen.

"Why don't we ask Napoleon where it is?" said Jennifer. But every time they went over to the bird man the raven flew away.

Jennifer's birthday was the last Saturday in March. Her mother woke her early. Mrs. Mace's eyes were shining. "Daddy's got something for you, Jenny," she said.

Jennifer jumped out of bed. She knew what she wanted, but she hadn't dared to ask for it.

Mr. Mace came into the bedroom. He was wheeling a beautiful, shining, brand new bicycle. It was bright blue and had *Jennifer* on the name plate on the handlebars.

Jennifer threw her arms around her father. She was too happy to say anything.

## 13

JENNIFER couldn't wait to show Mike the bicycle. She rode over to his house and left the bicycle on the front walk. She climbed the steps to the porch and rang the doorbell.

Mike's mother opened the door. "Hello, Jennifer," she said. "Are you looking for Mike? I thought he went over to your house." Mrs. Stewart caught sight of the shiny bicycle. "It's your birthday, isn't it?

Many happy returns of the day. Is that a birthday present?"

"Yes," Jennifer said. "I wanted to show it to Mike."

"Wait a minute," said Mrs. Stewart. "My mother has something for you too. Keep an eye on your bicycle." She went back into the house.

A minute later Mike's grandmother came to the door. She handed Jennifer a cardboard box. "Happy birthday," she said. "I baked you some cookies. Don't let Mike eat them all. Give some to your friend, the bird man." Mrs. Craig smiled and shut the door.

Jennifer decided to go home and see if Mike were waiting for her there. She balanced the box of cookies on her handlebars and rode around the corner to the apartment house. She took the bicycle up in the elevator.

"Did Mike come to call for me?" she asked her mother.

"No," said Mrs. Mace. "I thought you two would go bicycling together."

Jennifer went to her room. Where could Mike be? She sat on her bed and opened the box of cookies. Just as she started to eat one something rattled the window pane. It must be the wind, thought Jennifer. She finished her cookie and took another. Again the window pane rattled. This time it sounded as if someone were tapping on it. Jennifer went to see.

A small brown pigeon was perched on the sill outside the window. He was pecking at the glass.

Jennifer opened the window. "Mike!" she said. "Is it you?"

"It's me all right," he cooed. "Were you expecting some other pigeon?"

"Oh, Mike, what have you done? You know we promised Napoleon we wouldn't go into his tree any more."

"I didn't mean to," Mike said. "It was

an accident. I was trying to rig up a trapeze for Napoleon on the clothesline when I slipped and fell into the tree."

The pigeon hopped into the room. He fluttered from the windowsill to the top of the dresser and then on to the bed. "Happy birthday, Jen," he said. "Where'd you get the cookies? They look just like the kind my grandmother makes." He picked up a cookie in his claws and pecked at it. "Taste like them too."

"They are your grandmother's," Jennifer said. "She gave them to me for my birthday."

"She sure likes you," Mike said. "What else did you get for your birthday, Jen?"

"A bicycle," Jennifer said. "I thought we could go bicycling in the park, but now look at you!"

"It's not so great being a bird all by myself," Mike said. "If you want to ride your new bike I'll change back." He ate the last crumb of his cookie and flew to the window. "Meet me in front of the building."

Jennifer went to get her jacket. She filled the pockets with cookies. Then she took the bicycle down to the street again. Mike was perched on the brick gatepost in front of the door. He flew toward the park, and Jennifer pedaled after him. The sun was warm, and a little breeze blew through her hair. She felt as if she were flying too.

The big tree was standing by the park bench. Napoleon sat on one of the top branches. He flapped down onto the back of the bench to talk to them. "I had an idea you'd be back soon. I suppose you want a beech nut?"

"Yes," said the pigeon, flying down to perch beside the big bird. "Jennifer wants to go bike-riding, and it's more fun with two."

Napoleon flew off the bench onto the walk beside the bicycle. He walked slowly around it and gave it a poke or two with his beak. "I've seen these things," he said. "They're not bad if you don't have wings. This is a nice one." He looked with approval at the shiny new bicycle.

Mike flew up into the beech tree. It was all covered with little crinkly green leaves. They were damp and new and shone in the morning sunlight.

The pigeon hopped from branch to branch, looking under the leaves. "I can't find a nut," he said at last.

"There aren't any left on the tree," the raven said. "There won't be any more till fall."

"There must be some." Jennifer left the bicycle by the bench and walked over to the tree. "I think I see one up on that branch."

"Where?" Mike asked.

Jennifer pointed to a cluster of leaves. "I don't see any nuts," Mike told her.

Jennifer caught hold of the lowest

branch and pulled herself up into the tree. She climbed up to the branch she had pointed out. "Here, look," she said. She grabbed what looked like a nut. It was only a brown old leaf, and it crumbled to dust in her hand.

Napoleon had been sitting on the seat of the bicycle, trying to figure out how to

make it go. Suddenly he flew into the air with a loud squawk. Jennifer and Mike looked to see what was the matter.

A boy had come quietly over to the bicycle. When the raven flew off the seat he got on it. Now he was riding away at top speed.

"Stop!" Jennifer yelled. "That's my bike!" The boy only pedaled faster. By the time she had climbed down from the tree the bicycle was out of sight.

## 14

"OH, Mike, what shall I do?" Jennifer turned to look at the pigeon. She couldn't see him anywhere. She sat down on the bench and tried to blink the tears out of her eyes, but they kept coming. Jennifer put her hands over her eyes to hide the tears. She didn't want anybody to see her crying.

Someone sat down beside her. Jennifer took her hands away from her eyes. She looked into the kind old face of the bird man. His hat was a beautiful spring green. The raven was perched on top of it.

"Where's the tree?" Jennifer asked.

The old man smiled.

All at once Jennifer understood. "*You* are the tree," she said.

"Yes," said the bird man. "I'm the tree."

Jennifer stared at him. She wasn't crying any more. After a moment she asked, "Are you a man who turns into a tree or a tree who turns into a man?"

"I'm a tree. I turn into a man when I can be more help to my friends that way. When the birds start building their nests I'll be a tree until the little ones learn to fly. If I turn into a man I can keep the eggs or baby birds in my pockets, but I don't like to do it. It bothers their parents. The only bird who doesn't get upset about it is Napoleon. He's known me such a long time."

The big bird stretched his neck and ruffled his feathers. "I don't like an overcoat pocket nearly as much as the hollow in a tree," he said, "but I take things as they come."

Jennifer felt in her pocket. "Do you like cookies?" she asked the bird man.

"Oh, yes," he answered, "but I don't often get them. I'm too busy feeding the birds to feed myself. And when the birds are asleep I can be a tree and get all my food from the ground. My roots go far down into the earth. I never get hungry, but I do like cookies."

Jennifer pulled a handful of Mike's grandmother's cookies out of her pocket. "These are good," she said. "Have some."

The bird man took a cookie and bit into it. "I haven't had any like these in years," he said. "A little Scotch girl used to bring them to me. I wonder what became of her."

"I think she grew up to be Mike's grandmother," Jennifer said. "Anyway, that's who gave me the cookies."

There was a whirring sound. The little brown pigeon flew down onto Jennifer's lap. He was out of breath from flying so fast. Jennifer picked him up. She could feel his heart thumping under the soft feathers.

"Mike! Where have you been?" she asked.

"I followed that boy who stole your bike," he said. "I found out where he lives. Come on, I'll show you."

Mike was too tired to fly any more. Jennifer carried him, and Mike told her which way to go. It was a long walk.

"I took short cuts when I was flying," Mike told her, "and cut out the corners."

They went around the lake and out of

the park on the other side. When they were some distance away from the park Mike pointed with his claw to a red brick apartment building. "He took the bike in there," he said.

Jennifer looked hard at the building. "It looks like the place where I was almost eaten," she said.

"Maybe it's the same kid," Mike said. "Do you remember which window you went in?"

Jennifer showed him a window on the corner of the top floor. "That one with the purple curtains," she said.

Mike fluttered out of her arms and flew up to the window. He perched on the sill and looked into the room. Then he flew back to Jennifer. "It's him all right. He's in there now trying to take the name plate off your bicycle."

"We've got to get up there and stop him." Jennifer tucked the bird into the front of her jacket. She went into the vestibule of the apartment building.

A lady with a baby carriage and an armload of groceries was stuck in the door to the lobby. Jennifer held the door open for her and then slipped through behind her. She followed her into the elevator. The lady got out with her carriage on the fourth floor. Jennifer pushed the button and went up to the sixth.

Jennifer walked over to the door of the apartment belonging to the people who had wanted to eat her. She took the pigeon out from under her jacket. After taking a deep breath Jennifer rang the doorbell.

The fat woman opened the door. She looked at Jennifer. "If you're selling cookies, I don't want any," she said. She caught sight of the pigeon. "Where'd you get that?"

"I found him," Jennifer said. "He seems

to be somebody's pet. I'm trying to find out where he belongs."

The fat woman smiled. "You came to the right place," she said. "He belongs to my boy." She called back over her shoulder, "Hey, Steve, come here!"

Steve came to the door.

"The little girl is returning your squab," his mother said.

Steve reached out to grab Mike, but the pigeon flew into the apartment and began flying from room to room.

"I'll help you catch him," Jennifer said. Before anyone could stop her, she ran into the apartment.

"Follow me, Jen. The bike is in here." Mike swooped through a doorway.

The blue bicycle was lying on its side on the floor. Jennifer picked it up. She began to roll it out of the room.

"What are you doing?" The fat woman rushed over to her.

"It's my bicycle," Jennifer said. She was frightened, but she wasn't going to let Steve or his mother know it.

"No, it isn't. It belongs to my boy. You're a thief. Get out of here."

Jennifer kept a tight grip on the bicycle. "It's a girl's bike, and it has my name on it."

Steve had come into the room. "Where has it got your name on it?" he asked.

Jennifer looked. The nameplate was gone.

Suddenly the pigeon whirred down and gave Steve a terrible peck on the hand. The boy screamed and dropped something. Mike caught it in mid-air. He flew round and round the room, knocking over lamps and sending dishes crashing from the table to the floor.

"It's the name plate, Jen. Take it," Mike said, as he flew over Jennifer's head.

She reached up and took the little metal

plate from the pigeon's claws. Then she held it up for the fat woman to see. "It says *Jennifer*. My father gave me the bicycle just this morning. I can prove it's mine."

Mike was having fun. He flew into the kitchen and knocked a box of cereal off the shelf. Corn flakes scattered across the floor. In the hall he swung on the pendulum of a cuckoo clock. The clock fell off the wall. Finally he came to rest on top of the purple curtains in the living room.

The boy Steve ran over and reached up to grab the bird. Mike dodged his fingers. He flew down and gave the boy a peck on first one ear and then the other.

Steve put up his hands to protect his face. "Mom," he screamed, "help me!"

Steve's mother rushed over to him, and Jennifer wheeled the bicycle to the door of the apartment. She rolled it out into the hall and held the door open for Mike to fly out. The elevator was still on the sixth floor. Jennifer got into it with the bicycle. The bird perched on the handlebars. They reached the ground floor and went out into the spring sunshine.

## 15

JENNIFER pedaled through the park. Mike sat on her handlebars so that he could talk to her. "We still have to turn me back to myself," he said.

Jennifer was so happy to get her bicycle back that she had forgotten Mike's problem. "There won't be any more beech nuts on the tree until fall," she reminded him. "We'd better ask the bird man what to do."

"Why the bird man?" Mike asked.

"Because *he* is the tree," Jennifer said. And then she told Mike all about it.

When they came to the lake they saw the big tree near the park bench. A lady was sitting on the bench. A little boy was playing with a pull toy. Next to him a baby sat in a stroller. The baby waved at two robins in the tree overhead. They were starting to build a nest.

There were a great many people in the park now. Teenagers walked hand in hand at the edge of the lake. Several boys were fishing. Three old ladies sat on a bench and gossiped. Jennifer had never seen so many dogs at one time. They raced in circles and barked at the horseback riders who came galloping along the bridle path.

"I don't think the tree will turn into the bird man with all this going on," Jennifer said. "He always does it when no one is looking."

Mike watched the robins working on their nest. "They're going to have that done in no time," he said.

"Yes," Jennifer agreed. "And then they'll lay eggs in it. The bird man will stay a tree until the baby birds fly away. That means we won't be able to talk to the bird man for ages."

Mike flew up into the tree to speak to the robins. Then he flew back to his perch on the handlebars of the bicycle. "Selfish birds!" he said. "I asked them to stop work for a while, but they wouldn't." His feathers drooped. "I'm hungry," he said.

Jennifer pulled the last cookie out of her pocket and gave it to him. Mike held the cookie in the claws of one foot and pecked at it. "Nothing like these," he said.

Mike was cheerful again, but Jennifer reminded him, "Your folks will worry about you."

"You can telephone my mother and tell her I'm eating lunch at your house," Mike said.

When Jennifer reached home she took the bicycle up in the elevator. Mike flew up to her windowsill.

Jennifer's mother was waiting for her. "Jenny," she said. "Why don't you ask Mike to have dinner with us tonight?

We'll have a little birthday party. I'm going to bake a cake. What kind would you like?"

"A yellow cake with chocolate icing," Jennifer said, "but I'm not sure if Mike can come. I'll ask him." She wondered if pigeons liked chocolate icing. She was pretty sure that this one did, but she didn't know if her mother would want a pigeon eating at the same table with her.

"I bought a bag of peanuts," Mrs. Mace said. "If you go to the park after lunch you can take them along for the squirrels."

"Could I have some now, Mother? There's a hungry pigeon on my windowsill."

"Oh dear. Pigeons are such dirty birds."

"No they're not, Mother. Anyway, not this one. He's a nice little bird. Come and see." Jennifer took her mother's hand and pulled her into the bedroom.

Mike was waiting on the windowsill. When Jennifer opened the window he hopped into the room. He sat on the dresser top and cocked his head on one side.

Mrs. Mace stared. "He *is* a nice little bird," she said. "Do you really think he would eat a peanut?"

"I've seen him eat them before," Jennifer said. "Where are they? I'll get them."

"They're in the kitchen cabinet," Mrs. Mace said. Jennifer ran to get the peanuts for her mother.

While her mother was busy feeding the pigeon Jennifer slipped out of the room. The telephone was in the kitchen. Jennifer dialed Mike's number.

His mother answered the phone. "Mike is eating lunch at my house," Jennifer told her. "And is it all right if he has supper here too? My mother is going to bake a birthday cake."

"Of course Mike can have supper with you, Jennifer," Mrs. Stewart said. "How were the cookies?"

"Great," Jennifer told her. "They're all gone now."

"I thought they would be," Mike's mother said. "Well, have a good time." She hung up the telephone.

Jennifer went back into the bedroom. Mike was sitting on her mother's shoulder cooing to her. The top of the dresser was covered with peanut shells.

## 16

AFTER lunch Jennifer noticed that the sky had begun to cloud over. She took the rest of the bag of peanuts and walked toward the park. Mike flew out of the bedroom window and joined Jennifer as she went through the park gate. He perched on her shoulder.

A gray squirrel sat on one of the branches of an oak tree. Jennifer stood under the tree and held out a peanut. The squirrel crawled down the trunk until he could reach the nut. Then he climbed back up to the branch to eat it.

"He's afraid to come down with all the dogs around," cawed a voice from higher up in the tree. Jennifer looked up to see the raven. "I've been trying to get him to dig up one of the beech nuts he buried last winter," the raven said.

"Couldn't he point to where he hid them?" Jennifer asked. "Then we could dig one up."

"He says he doesn't remember where they are until he smells them, but they're all over the place," Napoleon told her. "If you were underground you'd be sure to find one."

"Underground!" Mike fluttered off Jennifer's shoulder to perch beside the raven. "Don't you remember that we were nearly trapped there last winter?"

"I just thought I'd mention it," the raven said. "But never mind, there'll be lots of beech nuts in the fall."

Jennifer walked over to the shore of the lake. There was a crowd of boats on the water. She saw Susan who sat behind her in school. Susan was in a rowboat with her sister and brother. Susan waved to her. "Want a ride?" she called.

Jennifer looked around for Mike. He had fluttered out of the oak tree and flew past her. "Get them to take you to the island, Jen," he said. "I'll wait for you there."

"Come on, Jennifer," Susan called again. "We have lots of room." The rowboat pulled over to the stone rim of the lake.

Jennifer stepped into the boat and sat down beside Susan. "Thank you," she said. "I love boat rides."

Susan's brother rowed out into the center of the lake. The boat passed five white ducks swimming in a row. There wasn't a sea gull to be seen.

Jennifer was wondering how she could ask to be let off at the island when Susan's big sister gave her a shove.

"Quick, get down in the boat, Jennifer! There's the man who rents out the boats. He'd better not see you."

Jennifer crouched on the floor of the boat. "What's wrong with me being in the boat?" she asked.

"We only paid for three people," Susan's sister explained.

"Why don't you let me off on the island?" said Jennifer.

Susan's brother rowed the boat to the shore of the island. "How will you get back to the mainland?" he asked.

"I know a way," Jennifer said, and she stepped out of the boat into the long grass.

Mike was waiting on the twig of a bush. "Let's get going. It's starting to rain." He flew onto her shoulder.

Jennifer didn't want to go underground again, but Mike didn't seem to be afraid. She didn't want him to know that she was. And it seemed as if this was the only way to turn him into himself again. She started pushing her way through the grass.

The grass wasn't frozen any longer. Green shoots were mixed with the brown. The ground was soft and muddy underfoot. There was a fresh smell of growing plants. Jennifer parted the damp weeds with her hands and made a path between them.

The grass and weeds became taller, and soon they were walking through the tunnel. The light was a brighter green than Jennifer remembered.

Mike turned his little head and looked around. "We're coming to the upside-down trees, Jen," he said. "Look, everything is moving!"

Jennifer looked. All the little grubs and

worms were crawling around in the roots. A field mouse scampered above them. The roots themselves were waving around, getting longer and longer. "They're growing," Jennifer said. "Do you see any beech nuts, Mike?"

The pigeon flew off her shoulder and fluttered between the curling roots. "Here's one," he said. He grabbed it in his claws and brought it down to Jennifer.

She looked at the nut. "This one has sprouted, Mike," she said. "There's nothing left to eat in the shell. See if you can find another."

Mike flew back into the moving jungle. He dodged between the twisted roots. "There are a lot of beech nuts," he called to Jennifer, "but they're all starting to grow." He untangled himself from a long tendril. "I'm afraid I'll get stuck here. Everything seems to want to catch me." He flew back to Jennifer's shoulder.

They had come to the huge upside-down tree. Jennifer saw the little hole far above. "Stay close to me, Mike," she said. She began to climb up through the maze of roots. "We're right under the beech tree," she said. "Look, Mike, here's a nut that isn't sprouting."

"Give it to me," the pigeon said. "I'd better eat it before it decides to grow."

"Would you mind getting off my shoulder first?" Jennifer said.

The pigeon flew onto a tree root, and Jennifer cracked open the beech nut shell.

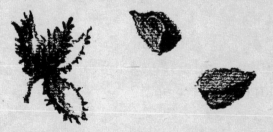

She gave Mike one of the little nuts. He ate it and opened his beak for another. Jennifer popped it into the beak.

A moment later she saw Mike hanging on to the root by his hands. "It's slippery," he said. "It's wetter in here than I remember."

Water was dripping down among the roots. The air began to turn to a fine mist. Jennifer and Mike could hardly see the hole above them. They felt as if they were climbing through mud. It was easier than pushing through hard ground, but it was messy. Jennifer wondered why she had ever thought it was fun to play with mud. She felt it in her hair, her ears, under her fingernails, and just about everywhere else.

At last she came to the hole in the ground and wiggled up through it. Mike slithered after her.

**17**

IT was raining hard. There were no people left in the park. Mike and Jennifer were once more under the magic tree. The big raven flapped down out of the branches.

"I was beginning to worry about you," he said. "If I'd known it was going to rain I never would have suggested that you go underground. You might have drowned."

The rain felt good after all the mud. Jennifer turned her face up to the sky. "I'm so glad to be out of there," she said. "I don't ever want to go back."

Mike stretched his arms and wiggled

his fingers. "It was fun being a bird," he said.

Napoleon nodded. "That's what I think," he said. "But remember, you promised you'd stay out of the hole in the tree. I've been thinking of building a big nest that will block up that hole. I know it would please my bride."

"Caw!" agreed a voice from the tree.

Jennifer and Mike looked up. Another raven was perched on one of the upper branches.

Mike started to walk toward the gate of the park. "Come on, Jen," he said. "Didn't you say your mother was going to bake a cake?"

Jennifer started to run. She called back over her shoulder, "First one home licks the bowl!"